READING FOR INDEPENDENCE | CURRICULUM FOUNDATION SERIES

REG. U.S. PAT. OFF.

THE NEW TALL TALES

Revised Edition

PART TWO

Marion Monroe
A. Sterl Artley

Advisor, Helen M. Robinson

Illustrator, Connie Moran

Scott, Foresman and Company
Chicago Atlanta Dallas Palo Alto Fair Lawn, N.J.

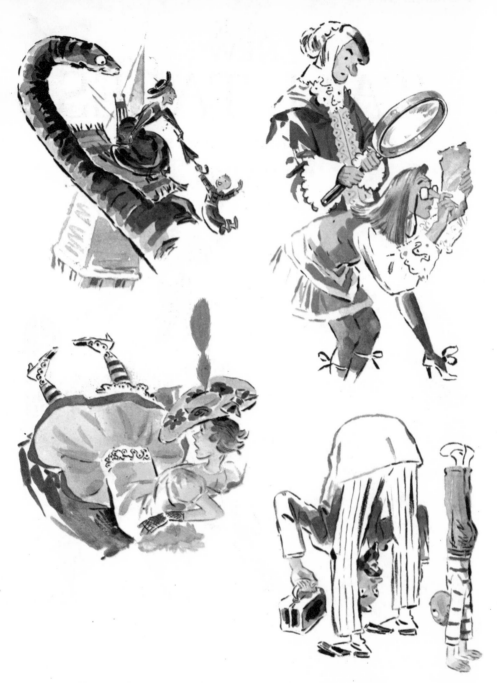

Tales

Flyaway at the Air Circus

A new little airplane named Flyaway sat on the ground at the airport. He stretched his new red wings in the sun. He turned his new red nose skyward to watch some planes that were flying high in the air.

"Tomorrow," cried Flyaway, "I'll be up there, too! Oh, I hope I can remember all I was taught about flying."

Just then a large silvery plane rolled off the runway near Flyaway. The large plane stopped and called, "Hello there, stranger! Have you been around here before?"

"No, Passenger Plane," replied Flyaway. "I just came from the factory. I was rushed here to help with tomorrow's events."

Mail Plane rolled along just then. He was getting ready to take off.

"Don't go yet!" shouted Passenger Plane to Mail Plane. "Tell me what's going on here tomorrow!"

"Air circus," roared Mail Plane. And off toward the runway he sped.

"Well, well!" exclaimed Passenger Plane. "Pump up my tires! An air circus!"

Then he called to another plane standing nearby, "Say, Jet, do you know anything about the air circus?"

"I'm performing in it," replied Jet.

"I'm going to take up some parachute jumpers," said Army Plane.

"I'm going to do some stunts in the water," said Seaplane.

Flyaway could not be still another minute. He bounced up and down on his fat little wheels, and he shouted as loud as he could to the other airplanes.

"Listen to me, fellows!" cried Flyaway. "I'm going to do a stunt for the air circus tomorrow, too. I'm going to write words in the sky. I'm a skywriter, I am! I'm a high skywriter."

"Well, well! Wiggle my rudder!" said Passenger Plane. "A little fellow like you flying at such a high altitude and writing in the sky. That's just marvelous! What are you going to write?"

"I heard someone at the factory say I'd write WELCOME TO THE AIR CIRCUS!" answered Flyaway. "This is my first job, and I just can't wait for tomorrow to come. Tomorrow I'll write words high in the sky for all the people to see."

Passenger Plane said, "Well, propel my propellers! I'm really going to be proud of you tomorrow."

The next afternoon there was a huge crowd at the airport to see the circus.

Flyaway was ready to do the first stunt. His gas tank was full of gas. His other tank was full of oil for smoke writing. His motor throbbed. Flyaway was terribly excited.

Down the long runway he sped. He lifted his tail and pushed off into the air.

"Oh!" the little plane shouted happily. "I do remember the lessons I learned about flying."

Flyaway flew higher and higher. Before long he looked like a tiny red spot in the sky. "I'm high enough for the stunt," he thought.

Suddenly a puff of white smoke shot out behind the little red plane.

"My, that's pretty!" exclaimed Flyaway. "Now I'll write WELCOME."

Flyaway danced through the air, spiraling and diving. Then he looked back to see what he had written.

"Dear me!" gasped the little red plane. "Something's dreadfully wrong!"

The curly ribbon of white smoke behind Flyaway did not look a bit like WELCOME.

The little plane tried again. He banked and turned and did a roll-over. But he made only white smoke squiggles in the sky.

"Oh-h-h!" moaned Flyaway. "This is horrible. I learned to fly, but I didn't learn how to write! What shall I do?"

Flyaway thought of all the people waiting to see him write WELCOME. He thought of Passenger Plane who had said he would be proud. Then Flyaway felt depressed.

Sadly he gazed at the squiggly white smoke. Suddenly he had a tremendous idea. If he couldn't write, he'd draw pictures.

Off streaked Flyaway to a nice clean spot of blue sky. "I'll draw a dog," he decided. "Everybody likes dogs."

Flyaway zoomed through the air—up and around and around. Then he floated down so that he could look up at his picture.

He saw a curly poodle dog about a mile high. But it did not have a short poodle-dog tail. Its tail was two or three miles long.

Flyaway raced across the sky, leaving another white streak behind him. "Well!" he cried. "That looks like a clothesline! I'll make the longest clothesline in the world. And I'll hang great big socks and shirts and pajamas on my clothesline."

When the line was full of clothes, Flyaway flew over to join some clouds.

"Hold still," he said to a cloud. He sped around it a few times. Suddenly the cloud looked like a snowman with a pipe in his mouth and a hat on his head.

Just then Flyaway noticed that he was out of writing smoke. He could not make another white wisp in the sky. Now he must go back to the airport.

Flyaway landed on the runway. Someone rolled him into a hangar and closed the doors.

All alone in the dark, the little plane felt forlorn. "What will people think of me? How can I ever face Passenger Plane? I'll never be hired again to do any skywriting. Maybe I'll never even fly again."

Sad little Flyaway remained in the hangar the rest of the afternoon. He grew more downhearted by the minute.

Just at sundown he heard someone opening the hangar doors. Suddenly a man rushed into the hangar and rolled Flyaway outside. To Flyaway's amazement, crowds of people were standing outside the hangar.

Flyaway heard shouts. "Hurray! Three cheers for Flyaway!"

"Cheers for me?" wondered Flyaway.

A little girl hung a wreath on his propeller. Then she gave Flyaway a pat and kissed him on his bright red nose.

Finally the crowd left. Flyaway heard Passenger Plane say, "Drain my gas tank! You were the best part of the circus!"

"I was supposed to write words, not draw pictures," said Flyaway sadly.

Passenger Plane said, "It wasn't your fault you hadn't learned to write. And you used your head very cleverly. That's what counts."

"Well, thanks," said Flyaway. "But I do want to learn to write, and someday I will."

Questions

1. What did Passenger Plane mean when he said Flyaway had used his head cleverly?

2. How many syllables do you hear in marvelous? in parachute? in altitude? Which syllable is accented in all these words?

3. Say the words marvelous and parachute. In which do you hear the vowel of car in the accented syllable? Do you hear the vowel of all or of hat in the accented syllable of altitude?

William

William was a goat with a long thin wisp of whiskers. He was a grouch, and he had a grouchy look.

Farmer Brown, who was William's master, had long thin whiskers, too. He looked even grouchier than William.

The goat admired Farmer Brown. He often thought, "If I had shoes, my master and I would look very much alike."

One day William was trotting along a dusty country road, thinking about shoes. He was wondering how he could get a pair when he met a tailor. The tailor was carrying a stylish suit of clothes he had just made.

"Sir!" called William in a voice that was very polite for him. "Please make me some shoes so I will look like Farmer Brown."

The tailor squinted his eyes and looked William over. Then he scratched his head and said, "I can make you a coat, or a pair of britches, or a vest. But——"

"Butt me no butts!" cried William most impolitely. "That's a fighting word!" And he butted the tailor into a shallow ditch.

Then, tossing his wispy whiskers, grouchy old William trotted on down the dusty road. He had not gone far when he met a pretty milliner. She was wearing a hat that she had just made, and she was very proud of it. The milliner's hat had a lavender feather on it that showed which direction the wind was blowing. It could really be called a weather-vane hat.

"Lady! Lady!" called William. "Please make me some shoes so I will look like Farmer Brown."

The milliner tapped her dimpled cheek and frowned. At last she answered, "I can make you a hat," she said. "I can make you a hat like mine with a feather vane on it. Or I can make you a satin bonnet with velvet bows. But——"

"Butt me no butts!" shouted the goat in a loud, angry voice. William lowered his head and dumped the pretty milliner, weather-vane hat and all, into the ditch beside the road.

William gave his whiskers an angry toss. Then he trotted on down the road. Presently he met a man who was a carpenter.

"Man! Make me some shoes so I will look like my master!" William demanded. He was so cross by this time that he didn't say "please."

The carpenter was very much surprised. In a startled voice he said, "I can make you a house or a barn. I can make you a palace or a pigpen. But——"

"Butt me no butts!" snorted William. And he butted the carpenter into the ditch.

William tossed his whiskers and trotted on. The fourth person he met was a baker.

"Man!" shouted William. "Make me some shoes so I will look like Farmer Brown!"

The baker rubbed his forehead, leaving some flour on it. "I can make you some raisin cookies, a custard pie, or a wedding cake," he said. "But——"

"Butt me no butts!" screamed William. And he butted the baker into the ditch.

William trotted along the road, shaking his whiskers angrily. The expression on his face was now grouchier than ever.

The next person that William met was a shoemaker.

"Man!" bellowed William. "Will you make me a pair of shoes so I'll look like my master?"

The shoemaker was a very jolly fellow. He was much amused at the goat's request.

"That order is rather odd," he chuckled to himself. "But I could make this goat some sturdy shoes without much trouble. I could make him some high-button shoes."

Then the shoemaker beamed at William and said, "Very well! I'll make you some high-button——"

That is as far as the man got.

"Buttin'! Buttin'!" roared William. "I do the buttin'! That's my specialty!" And he butted the poor shoemaker into the ditch just as he had the tailor, the milliner, the carpenter, and the baker.

Then William trotted angrily down the dusty road.

So the grouchy old goat never did get his shoes, which perhaps served him right.

Questions

1. Why did William want shoes?

2. Do you think it served him right not to get them? Why, or why not?

3. Why do these words—<u>but</u> and <u>butt</u>, <u>button</u> and <u>buttin'</u>—make this story funny?

4. What is the root word in <u>stylish</u>? in <u>specialty</u>?

What suffix is added to each root word?

5. What prefix is added to the word <u>head</u> to make the word <u>forehead</u>?

The Palace Mystery

The King had on his best spectacles—the ones he wore only on Sundays and on state occasions. He was peering at a piece of paper covered with scribbles and scrawls.

He turned the paper this way and that way. He twisted his head that way and this way. Finally he picked up his everyday glasses and put them on over his best ones.

"Such scribbly writing!" he muttered. "I declare! I can't make out even one word of it!"

The King turned to his favorite servant. "Why can't people print if their writing is so awful?" the King complained. "I must make a law about that."

"My eyesight is very good," the servant said. "Perhaps I can read the writing."

The King handed him the paper, and the servant looked at it for a long time. He held it up to the light. He held it before a mirror in case the scribble was written backward. But he could not read a single word.

"All I can make out are a few commas," the servant remarked at last.

"They may not be commas," the King said. "They may be dots over *i*'s."

The King heaved a sigh. Then he said, "I don't suppose there's anyone in the palace who can read such scribbly writing, but I shall see."

He rang a bell, and a footman appeared at the door immediately.

"Ask all the noblemen to assemble in the throne room at once," the King commanded.

When the noblemen arrived, the King said, "Gentlemen! I have here a paper with some very scribbly writing on it. Can one of you read this sort of thing?"

All the noblemen peered at the writing. They twisted themselves this way and that. And they turned the paper that way and this. They looked at it through their spectacles and even studied it with magnifying glasses. But they could not read a word of it.

"Could it be secret ink?" one nobleman asked. "I'll hold the paper in front of the fire to see if the writing becomes clearer."

He held the paper near the fire until it was scorched. Still he could not make out a single letter of the scribbling.

Just then the servant had a brilliant idea. "I know!" he cried. "There's one person who can always read unreadable writing!"

"Who?" everyone asked at once.

"The clerk at the drugstore," answered the servant. "Doctors always use scribbly writing when they order pills and things."

So without delay the King, the servant, and all the noblemen went to the drugstore.

The King handed the paper to the clerk. "Can you read this writing?" he asked.

"One minute, Your Majesty!" cried the clerk. He rushed to the rear of the store and reappeared in half a minute.

"Well, my man," said the King, "were you able to read the scribbling?"

The clerk did not answer the question. He handed a small bottle and the paper to the King and said, "Ten cents, please." Then he sped away to wait on a customer.

The King, his favorite servant, and all the noblemen hurried back to the throne room in the palace. "That scribbling must have been a doctor's prescription," said the King. "Why else would the clerk give me this bottle of stuff? I think I'll try a small dose of it."

The King was just going to pull out the cork when he heard the blare of trumpets. The Queen was entering the throne room.

"Mercy! What's going on?" the Queen asked, staring at the crowd in the room.

"We had a mystery here," replied the King. "But it's solved now."

He held up the paper and the small bottle. "No one at the palace could read this scribbly writing," he explained. "So we took it to the clerk at the drugstore. He's good at reading scribbling. It was a doctor's prescription for this stuff. I'm going to take some."

The Queen grabbed the bottle, uncorked it, and sniffed. "This," she cried, "is mint! And it's mine! I told the clerk to have some of my favorite oil of mint ready today. He thought you had come for it."

Then the Queen grabbed the paper and waved it in the air. "And this," she said, "is not a doctor's writing!"

"It isn't?" cried the poor King in dismay. "Then there's still a mystery."

"Oh, no, there isn't," the Queen declared. "This is a letter from your Aunt Tilly. It says she is coming for a visit."

"How can you know that?" the King asked. "None of us could read the letter."

The Queen confessed, "I can't read it either. Nobody can ever read Aunt Tilly's scribbly writing. But I know it says she's coming for a visit."

The King looked so confused that the Queen explained, "Whenever I receive a letter I can't read, I know it's from Aunt Tilly. She never sends a letter unless she's coming to visit. So—there you are."

The King was pleased about the visit, and he was astounded at his wife's cleverness. "Lovely!" he cried. "Very lovely, indeed!"

Questions

1. What was the palace mystery?
2. Who solved it? How?
3. What had the King, the servant, and the noblemen done to try to solve the mystery?
4. Did the drugstore clerk have trouble reading the writing? Why, or why not?
5. Which of the words below are accented on the first syllable? the second syllable?

mystery   prescription   assemble
occasion   spectacles   magnify

What do you see in the spelling of each word that helps you know which vowel sound to try first in the accented syllable?

Cassy's Idea

One morning Cassy Tuttle spoke crossly to her husband. "Elmer!" she exclaimed. "You have to do an errand today. You must take corn to the mill to be ground. I can't bake corn bread without corn meal."

"Yes," Elmer agreed, "I should take corn to the mill and eggs and vegetables to market. But I can't possibly do it."

Then Elmer patiently began to explain. "You know I always used our old steer Felix and our young steer Hugo to pull the wagon. Now that old Felix is dead, it's impossible to take the wagon to town."

"I suppose so," said Cassy impatiently. "Still we must get corn meal somehow."

Elmer sat and thought out loud about the problem. "One steer can stand on only one side of the wagon tongue. He can hold up only one end of the wooden yoke."

Suddenly Cassy exclaimed, "Elmer! I have an idea! You take Felix's place and hold up one end of the yoke. You hitch Hugo to the wagon, and I'll hitch you to it. Both of you can pull the wagon to town!"

Elmer was not exactly pleased with his wife's idea. But neither was he displeased. So he agreed to try it.

Cassy grabbed up a basket of eggs and ran outside to set the basket in the wagon.

Elmer went to the barn and filled two sacks with corn. He set the sacks in the wagon to take to the mill. Next Cassy and Elmer picked basketfuls of radishes, tomatoes, beets, and other garden vegetables and set those baskets in the wagon.

Then Cassy rushed into the house to get her hat and purse. When she came out, Elmer had Hugo hitched to the wagon.

"It's a gorgeous day!" Cassy said gaily. "And it's going to be a pleasant trip."

"Maybe so," said Elmer. "Just maybe. Now, Cassy, hitch me to the wagon."

Cassy slipped the yoke over Elmer's head and set it on his shoulders. Then she tied Elmer to the wagon tongue with a rope.

"Now tie the knots good and tight," said Elmer. "Pleasant trip or not, I aim to stay with this rig till we get to town."

"You can't blame me if you don't," said Cassy as she gave the rope a last tug. Then she climbed onto the wagon seat.

"Giddap!" she called.

At first all went well with Elmer, Hugo, and the wagon. But when they reached the big dirt road, which was full of deep ruts, the wagon began to jolt and jerk.

When that happened, Elmer could not hold down his end of the yoke as Felix, the old steer, had always done. Elmer's end of the yoke flew up, and Elmer flew up with it. Every time Elmer and the yoke flew up, the wagon jerked forward and smacked against Hugo's bony hind legs.

All this did not seem quite right to Hugo, the young steer. Finally he got mad and started to gallop. Of course Elmer had to gallop, too.

"Whoa!" screamed Cassy. "Whoa, I say! Whoa, both of you!"

But the steer wouldn't stop, and Elmer couldn't. So on they galloped.

Poor Elmer clung to the yoke with one hand and to the wagon tongue with the other. His feet left the ground with each jolt of the wagon.

Hugo's hoofs stirred up clouds of dust
that almost suffocated Elmer. He gasped
and panted, and his face got red. But he
wasted enough breath to yell, "Cassy——
this——was——your idea!"

Suddenly Cassy saw that Elmer and Hugo were very close to a deep ditch. A few more inches and the wagon would upset.

Cassy knew that "Haw" meant to turn to the left. So she yelled, "Haw! Haw! Haw! Haw, Hugo! Haw, Elmer!"

After what seemed like ages, Hugo and Elmer swerved to the left, and the wheels of the wagon narrowly missed the ditch.

Hugo began to gallop faster and faster. Elmer's feet were off the ground most of the time.

"Cassy! Stop us!" Elmer pleaded.

Poor Cassy was helpless. She could do nothing but hold on. Luckily she didn't look at the back of the wagon. If she had, she'd surely have fallen off the wagon seat.

The egg basket was jouncing up and down, and every egg was smashed. The sacks of corn were scooting back and forth, spilling the corn right and left. There was a long trail of fresh garden vegetables behind the wagon.

What Cassy did see was even worse. The road curved to the right before it crossed the bridge over Mill Creek. But Hugo and Elmer had not veered to the right. They were headed straight for the creek.

"Turn to the right!" screamed Cassy. "Elmer! Hugo! Gee! GEE, I say!"

The pair turned to the right and got back on the road just in time to cross the bridge.

In another minute they reached town. In two more minutes they were galloping down the main street, making a frightful noise.

The town barber looked to see what was causing all the commotion. "A runaway!" he cried and ran out of his shop with a razor in one hand and a towel in the other. "Stop the runaways!" he shouted. "Stop them before they kill themselves!"

"Stop Hugo first!" Cassy screamed. "Elmer will be glad to stop by himself."

People dashed out of all the stores. They managed to head the runaways into a coal yard that had a high board fence around it.

At last Hugo and Elmer skidded to a stop. They were trapped.

When the people started to unyoke Elmer, he spluttered angrily at them. "Let——me be!" he gasped. "Unhitch——that steer. He's——he's the one——that——ran away. None of this——was my idea!"

"Oh, dear! That's right!" wailed Cassy, terrified by Elmer's gasping and the redness of his face. "It was my idea to hitch up Elmer and Hugo."

Finally Hugo and Elmer were unyoked. When poor Elmer had regained some of his strength, he found himself standing on the coal-yard scales.

Finally Elmer lost his temper. "Cassy!" he shouted. "You and your crazy ideas! Look what's happened to me. I've run off thirty pounds!"

Questions

1. What was Cassy's idea?

2. What did Elmer think of the idea at the beginning of the story?

How did he feel about it at the end of the story? Why?

3. How do you suppose Cassy felt at the end of the story? Why?

4. Why is this story called a tall tale?

5. What do the words <u>steer</u>, <u>tongue</u>, and <u>scales</u> mean in this story? What else can each of these words mean?

6. Look at the words below. What prefixes and suffixes do you see?

displease	redness	narrowly
basketful	regain	helpless
unhitch	bony	impatiently

Can you use each word in a sentence?

The Rocket That Ran Away

It was a cool day in early April. The big city park was deserted except for one man who was sitting on a bench, enjoying the sunshine. Presently he unfolded his newspaper and began to read it. The paper was full of stories about space ships and men from Mars and other planets.

The man did not see or hear anybody coming, but suddenly he felt a tap on his shoulder. The tapping felt as if it were done by something made of metal.

Horrified, the man thought, "A THING from Outer Space has landed here!"

The man swung around. Behind him stood a THING, but it was not from Outer Space. It was a timid-looking little rocket that was trembling with fear.

"P-p-please pardon me," it stuttered in a high, tinny voice. "I-I-I am in danger! P-please, can you hide me?"

"Of course," answered the man. "You can come right home with me. Nothing will harm you there."

He got up, refolded his newspaper, and held out his hand to the rocket. "Come with me," said the man.

"But, s-sir!" the rocket objected. "I can't be s-seen going along the s-street in daylight. They may be after me!"

The man said, "Don't be nervous. I'll wrap you in my paper and carry you under my arm. How will that be?"

The small rocket seemed to lose some of its fear. "That will be fine," it said.

So, with the rocket wrapped up and tucked snugly under his arm, the man walked home.

As soon as he was inside his front door, the man unwrapped the small rocket and set it down. "Here we are, safe and sound," the man said cheerfully. "Will you have some tea with me? Or perhaps you'd prefer some coffee or some orange pop."

"I'm afraid I only drink oil," replied the rocket. "I hope I'm not too much trouble."

"Oh, no, of course not," said the man. "I have some nice salad oil that I use on lettuce. I'll get you a cup of that."

In a little while the man was drinking tea, and the rocket was sipping oil and relaxing in a comfortable chair.

Before long the rocket spoke. "I'm sure you must be wondering why I wanted you to hide me," it said.

"Yes," the man replied. "I am curious."

The rocket blushed with shame and began to stutter. "The f-fact is, I f-found out that I was to be tested and fired today. So I ran away."

"Running away can't be such a terrible crime!" the man cried. "After all, there must be thousands of rockets to be fired."

"Oh, yes," sighed the rocket. "I have l-lots of rocket friends who think being tested and fired is quite enjoyable. It's—it's just that it's unheard of for a rocket to avoid being fired. I'm so ashamed!"

"There, there," said the man, giving the rocket a friendly smile. "Perhaps you'd like to tell me just why you ran away."

"Well," said the rocket with a sigh, "it embarrasses me to say so. But I'm different from all the other rockets. Something is wrong with me. It's——"

The little rocket leaned forward and said each part of a big word slowly and distinctly. "Ac-ro-pho-bi-a. I suffer from acrophobia."

"No!" the man cried. "Not acrophobia! That's unbelievable for a rocket!"

"But it's true," whispered the rocket. "I'm terribly afraid of high places."

For a minute the man looked startled. Then he grinned and said, "I'm afraid of high places, too. Why don't you live here with me from now on? With you to help me and me to help you, maybe we'll succeed in getting over our fear."

Questions

1. What does acrophobia mean? If you are not sure, read the top part of this page again. The rocket explains what the word means.

2. Why is it peculiar for a rocket to suffer from acrophobia?

3. What things in this story could really have happened? What things could only be in a make-believe story?

More Is Better

Abner Toggle lived all alone, and so he cooked his own meals.

One morning as Abner was eating toast and marmalade, he thought, "I'm tired of store-bought bread. I'd like some homemade bread. It would be a treat."

Just then Abner got an idea. "Maybe I could bake bread. I'm a pretty good cook."

He sprang up from the table and got his cookbook off the shelf. Then he looked up BREAD and read the directions.

"Well," said Abner, "this sounds simple. Now if I use twice as much flour and yeast and all these other things—and if I take twice as much care doing the things I'm supposed to do—I ought to have a huge batch of extra-good bread. I'll try it!"

Abner used twenty cups of flour instead of ten. He used four cakes of yeast instead of two. He used twice as much of everything as the book called for.

The directions said to sift the flour five times. So Abner did it ten times. All that sifting wore out his flour sifter.

Next he mixed everything together in a huge bowl. Abner stirred and stirred and stirred—twice as much as the cookbook said. Then he put the good-smelling batch of bread into a washtub to rise.

It took a long time for the bread to rise to the top of the big washtub, but it finally rose. Then Abner made the bread into plump loaves and put them into greased pans.

The bread had to rise once more before it would be ready for the oven.

Abner's bread was just ready to bake when a rap came at the door. It was Tuck Smith, the man who sold bread to Abner.

"Tuck!" cried Abner. "I neglected to tell you that I don't need bread. I'm baking my own. It's in the oven now."

Tuck looked disgusted. "I can imagine what your bread will taste like!" he snorted.

"Come back shortly and find out," Abner said. "It'll be extra good."

Tuck was very much annoyed. "I may never come back," he retorted. I've been going out of my way for years to bring bread to you, and now you start baking your own!" With a slam of the door, Tuck Smith left.

Abner went back to his bread-baking. "I'll have to have an extra-big fire to bake extra-good bread," he said to himself.

Then he added more fuel to the fire in the cookstove. Next he stuck his pans of bread into the oven and closed the door tight.

Before long the mouth-watering smell of baking bread filled the kitchen.

Abner glanced out the screen door and saw someone standing by the gate. It was a tramp, and he looked half starved.

"I smelled your bread," the tramp called. "Could I have a slice or two?"

"Of course," replied Abner, who was a very generous person. "But you will have to wait. My bread isn't done yet."

Just then Frank Twitter, Abner's nearest neighbor, drove up. He said, "We smelled your bread clear over at our place. We're out of bread. Would you lend us a loaf?"

"Be glad to," answered Abner. "But you will have to come in and wait. The bread isn't done."

Next a truck with two men in it stopped. "I'll take some of that good-smelling bread," the driver called. Then he added, "I didn't know there was a bake shop on this road."

"There isn't," Abner answered. "I was baking bread just for myself. But I made several loaves. So I can let you have one if you want to wait till they're done."

Abner went in the house and peeked into the oven. There sat sixteen loaves of bread. They were light golden-brown in color.

"My extra-good bread must be extra brown," thought Abner. So he stirred up the fire.

Meanwhile a funny thing had happened outside. When the oven door was open, the delicious odor of baking bread had poured out of the kitchen. Immediately three cars had braked to a stop near Abner's gate.

That was only the beginning. When Abner joined Frank in the yard, there were cars, trailers, trucks, bicycles, and moving vans parked near the fence.

"My lands!" said Abner. "People for miles around must have smelled my bread."

"Seems like it," Frank agreed. Then he asked, "Isn't that bread of yours taking an extra-long time to bake?"

Before Abner could answer, Tuck Smith drove up and leaped out of his car. He was waving a scrap of paper and a fountain pen.

"Glad you came back," called Abner.

Tuck shouted, "I came back for something important! I smelled your bread, and I saw people flocking here to smell it and probably buy some. Right then I had an idea."

Tuck ran up to Abner and explained, "We could make money by being partners. With you to make bread and me to sell it, we'd be a real success. I can see our sign now— SMITH AND TOGGLE BAKE SHOP."

"Not so fast," Abner replied. "Not so fast. A partnership requires some thought."

"Why think?" asked Tuck. "Just sign this paper that says we're partners."

Suddenly a shout came from the crowd. "The bread, Grandpop! Go look at it!"

Abner ran toward the house.

Clouds of extra-black smoke were pouring from the kitchen. Inside the oven Abner's bread was burned almost to cinders.

Sadly Abner took a panful outside to show to the crowd. Just as sadly the people left. Frank and Tuck went along with all the rest.

Abner Toggle knew what had been wrong with his idea for making extra-good bread. But he never admitted to anyone that twice as much doesn't always make things better.

If anyone asks Abner why he has never again baked bread, he just grins. Then he says, "My flour sifter is worn out."

Questions

1. Finish each of these sentences.

Abner Toggle baked bread because

He sifted the flour ten times because

He made an extra-big fire because

His bread was no good because

2. Which words below are accented on the first syllable? on the second syllable?

simple	annoy	sentence
neglect	admit	success
disgust	partner	Abner
cinder	fountain	require

What do you see in the spelling of each word that helps you know which vowel sound to try first in the accented syllable?

Westley Riggs Thinks

It was Friday morning, and Westley Riggs was almost ready to start to school. "Has anybody seen my thinking cap?" he called.

"What cap?" asked his mother.

"My thinking cap," Westley repeated. "Mrs. Marble said that we had to wear our thinking caps in her third grade. I didn't even have a thinking cap. So I made one. I made it out of paper that's hard to see. It just makes my hair look kind of shiny. Now I can't find that thinking cap."

His mother said, "I haven't seen it, and there isn't time to search for it. Run on to school. You look plenty shiny to me."

Westley was in his seat in Mrs. Marble's third-grade room when the last bell rang.

Mrs. Marble said, "Children! Today is teachers' visiting day. Company is coming to see us. We're going to give a program in the gym for our visitors."

"Oh!" gasped the pupils all together.

Mrs. Marble looked around the room. Then she said, "Westley Riggs looks so spick-and-span today that he can lead you to the gym. Now march quietly! Do exactly what Westley does!"

She gave Westley's head a pat before she hurried downstairs to greet the visitors.

Westley shook his head. The whole room had suddenly grown crooked. The walls and desks were crooked. The writing on the blackboard seemed to zigzag up and down.

Westley bumped his crooked way into the hall. The other children bumped after him. They were doing exactly what Westley did.

"Cut it out!" Roy Burd whispered.

"I can't help it!" wailed poor Westley.

Just then, with a loud crash, he tumbled head over heels downstairs. He landed, unhurt, in the middle of a group of visitors. Right behind him came all the other pupils, imitating everything that Westley did.

"Stop showing off!" Mrs. Marble ordered. "Follow Westley to the gym."

"Westley, stop it!" hissed Sarahlee Martin. "You're walking backward, and so are we!"

"It help can't I," moaned Westley, talking backward, too. "Do I can what?"

The entire third grade came marching into the gym, walking backward! They sat down in their seats backward!

People all over the gym said things like "Well, I never!" and "How ridiculous!"

Mrs. Marble did her best to pretend that nothing strange was going on. "Westley will lead our group in singing," she announced.

She leaned over and rumpled Westley's hair, none too gently. "Behave yourself," she whispered. "March the class up front."

"My head——" Westley began. Then he noticed that he was not talking backward and that he was facing the front of the room. So he quickly led the class onto the platform.

Mrs. Marble rushed up to hand Westley a baton to lead the singing. In her haste she brushed his head with the baton.

Suddenly Westley started to do strange things again. He turned upside down and stood on his hands, and so did the rest of the class.

"Oh!" cried Westley. "What shall I do?"

Mrs. Marble did the only thing she could think of. "Stand up!" she said to her pupils. "School is over for today. Class dismissed."

The other children raced out of the gym, leaving Westley upside down on the stage.

"Westley, stand up!" ordered the teacher. She gave his shoe sole a rap with her pencil.

Westley wailed, "I can't, Mrs. Marble."

She grabbed his legs and tried to tip him forward. But whoops! back he went again.

"This is an emergency!" the teacher cried. "I'll get the principal."

"Something is definitely wrong," said the principal when he saw Westley. "I'll get the doctor!"

When the doctor arrived, he leaned way over and looked at Westley's face. Then he asked Westley to stick out his tongue.

"This young fellow doesn't look sick," the doctor declared. "He doesn't need me. He needs an acrobat who can stand on his head and talk things over."

The principal said, "It just happens that I am an acrobat in my spare time. I'll go get into my costume. Wait right here."

"What else can I do?" Westley mumbled.

A moment later Mr. and Mrs. Riggs arrived. Sarahlee had run all the way to their house to tell them about Westley.

"Sarahlee was right!" Mrs. Riggs cried.

Mr. Riggs shouted, "Get to your feet, boy! How did you get in this predicament?"

"I don't know," said Westley with a sob. "Everything's gone wrong today. First, things were crooked. Then they were all backward. And now they're upside down!"

Just then the principal, dressed in tights, bounded onto the stage.

"Who are you?" Mr. Riggs shouted at the principal.

"He's the principal!" gasped Mrs. Marble.

Westley cried, "He *was* the principal! Now he's an acrobat. He's going to stand on his head and talk things over with me."

"This is no time for conversation!" roared Mr. Riggs. "You should be turned upright."

"That's been tried," said the principal. "It didn't last."

"Then think, Westley, think!" bellowed Mr. Riggs. "Use your head."

"I am," sobbed Westley.

His arms wobbled just then, and thump! his head hit the floor. Something almost like a shadow slipped off his head.

Slowly Westley turned right side up.

"Look," he said, pointing at the floor. "There's my thinking cap! I bet that old cap has been on my head all day."

His mother gave a shrill scream. "Don't touch it!" she cried. "That cap may have been the cause of all your troubles."

"Why, sure!" shouted Westley. When the cap was crooked, everything was crooked. When it was twisted around backward, why, everything was backward. When it flipped upside down, I flipped upside down, too."

Then Westley giggled. "Just think," he exclaimed, "what would have happened if my thinking cap had ever turned inside out!"

Questions

1. Who was the main character in this story? What caused each of his troubles?

2. Writers use many different words that mean "said." Here are some that were used in this story.

mumbled	shouted	gasped	bellowed
repeated	moaned	sobbed	whispered

Which words might tell you that someone spoke softly? loudly? angrily? sadly?

Which tells you that someone is surprised? that someone has said the same thing before?

3. How many syllables do you hear in the word <u>conversation</u>? in <u>predicament</u>?

The Machine

"Machines and I understand each other," Mr. Fuddle always boasted to Mrs. Fuddle. "I don't have to turn knobs, push switches, or press buttons. I just say GO, and they go. When I say STOP, they stop. I have a brain that understands machines very well."

Mrs. Fuddle always nodded her head when Mr. Fuddle told her that. She believed anything he said about machines.

One day Mrs. Fuddle was washing dishes, and Mr. Fuddle was wiping them for her. All of a sudden Mrs. Fuddle spoke up.

"Could you turn one kind of machine into another kind of machine?" she asked.

"Oh, yes! I could do that easily," bragged Mr. Fuddle. "I understand machines."

"Well, then," said Mrs. Fuddle, "could you turn our old washing machine into a dishwashing machine? I'd love to have one for our anniversary."

"You shall have one," said Mr. Fuddle. "Don't you worry about that. I'll start to experiment on the machine right now. By the time our anniversary gets here, you'll have a brand-new dishwashing machine."

During the next few weeks Mr. Fuddle did nothing but work on the machine. He went into town almost every day to purchase new tools. At home he would settle down to his work, surrounded by wrenches, hammers, files, saws, and cogwheels.

He hammered and sawed and filed. He tightened things and loosened things. He connected things and disconnected things. He took the old machine apart and put it back together again at least sixty times.

On the Fuddles' anniversary Mr. Fuddle finally got the machine together in a way that exactly suited him.

Mr. Fuddle called Mrs. Fuddle to admire the dishwasher. "My dear!" he cried. "Let me introduce you to the finest dishwashing machine that was ever made!"

He stood for a moment, looking with pride at the dishwasher. Then he started picking up his tools.

"Now, cook us a fine big supper," he said. "Use all the pots and pans you can. We'll dine tonight without a thought for the dishes and kettles that must be washed."

That night the Fuddles sat down to a huge meal. Mr. Fuddle used a different dish for every single thing he ate. He wanted to have lots of dirty dishes so that the new machine would be put to a real test.

"Tonight," he kept repeating to his wife, "we don't have to think about how many dishes we use. Tonight we'll see the proof of my skill. My dishwasher will show that machines and I understand each other."

At last the turkey and stuffing, the mashed potatoes and gravy, the corn and beans, the chocolate cake and maple-nut ice cream, and the apple pie with cheese had all been eaten. Every dish in the cupboard had been used.

Mr. Fuddle cleared the table. Then he put a stack of dishes that were piled high with turkey bones into the dishwashing machine.

"This machine takes care of the garbage, too," he explained to his wife proudly.

Mr. Fuddle put soap into the machine and turned on the water. Then he stepped back.

"Go!" he commanded.

Mrs. Fuddle gave a little groan when the machine started. "It won't break my dishes, will it?" she asked anxiously. "We used all my best china tonight."

"No, no, my dear," answered Mr. Fuddle. "Your good dishes will be washed with perfect safety. Don't fret."

"And will the dishes come out sparkling clean?" Mrs. Fuddle inquired.

"Yes, indeed, my dear," said Mr. Fuddle. "Yes, indeed. The dishes will be washed once in soapy water and then rinsed twice in clear water. All very sanitary."

He pointed to the right side of the machine. "The clean dishes will come out on this tray," he explained. "The turkey bones will be tossed into that big garbage can on the left."

Mr. Fuddle was smiling happily. His dishwashing machine was really working.

"Now, watch," he said. "The clean dishes will soon——" Suddenly he stopped talking. The dishwashing machine was rattling and clanking. Something was going wrong!

China plates came flying out of the left side of the dishwasher. They landed in the garbage can and shattered.

At the same time turkey bones came out on the tray on the opposite side. They were shiny-clean bones that had been scrubbed in foaming soapsuds and rinsed twice in gallons of clear water.

"Stop, machine! Stop!" cried Mrs. Fuddle.

"Be patient, my dear," said Mr. Fuddle. "The dishwashing machine seems to be working backward now. It will do better soon, I'm sure. We must give it time to get adjusted."

But the machine did not do better. Dishes kept falling into the garbage can. Turkey bones, clean and gleaming, kept piling up in neat stacks on the tray. Finally Mr. Fuddle shouted, "I'll toss in the knives and forks and spoons. Maybe that will help."

He threw in the silver, but it did not help a bit. Knives, forks, and spoons were soon clanging on top of the broken dishes. Bones were still piling up on the dish tray.

"Put in the pans!" screeched Mrs. Fuddle. "Maybe they'll clog the machine."

Mr. Fuddle stepped toward the stove to pick up some kettles. "I'll try it," he cried. "I'll put in these big cooking pots."

Suddenly everything was quiet!

The machine had stopped.

"What made the machine stop? Did you do something to it?" Mr. Fuddle asked his wife. But the poor woman was too upset over her ruined china to answer.

So Mr. Fuddle took the silver out of the garbage can and dumped the turkey bones on the heap of broken dishes. Then he took the bones and dishes out to the trash bin.

All the time he was trying to figure out what had caused the machine to stop. "Just before it stopped I said I'd put in the pots," he mumbled. "Why would that stop it?"

Suddenly he shouted, "POTS! That's it!"

Mr. Fuddle rushed into the house yelling, "The word *pots* stopped the machine."

"I don't understand," wailed Mrs. Fuddle.

"Of course not, dear," said Mr. Fuddle. "I'll explain. The machine was working backward. So what did I have to do to stop it? I had to say *stop* backward. And what is *stop* spelled backward? POTS, my dear, POTS! This is proof that machines and I truly do understand each other."

Questions

1. How did Mr. Fuddle stop the machine? Why did the word *pots* stop it?

2. Which of these words would you use to tell what kind of person Mr. Fuddle was?

hard-working   patient   thoughtful
boastful   clever   pleasant

What part of the story helped you choose each word?

Which of the words would you use to tell what kind of person Mrs. Fuddle was?

Why would you use each word?

3. What could you see, hear, smell, or taste when you read about

Mr. Fuddle making the dishwasher?
the Fuddles eating their dinner?
the dishwasher working backward?

4. What is the root word in <u>knives</u>? in <u>sparkling</u>? in <u>cried</u>? in <u>bragged</u>?

How does the spelling of each root word change when the ending is added?

5. How many root words do you see in <u>soapsuds</u>? What is a word like this called?

Chester's Pet

It was a glorious autumn day! From high on the back of Bronto, his pet dinosaur, Chester Pokleberry sniffed the air.

"I do wish Mr. Tubbs were here and not traveling in far-off places!" he exclaimed. "Then something wonderfully exciting would be bound to happen today."

Bronto started to wag his enormous tail at the mention of Mr. Tubbs' name.

"Easy there, Bronto," warned Chester. "I know just how you feel. If Mr. Tubbs hadn't sent that box of rare bones to me, you wouldn't exist today. One minute I was looking at old dusty bones. And the next minute I was looking at you!"

Just then the mailman called to Chester, "Here's another package from Mr. Tubbs."

Hearing that name again made Bronto start toward the mailman.

Chester cried, "Don't be afraid of Bronto!"

"I'm not," said the mailman. "I like him. He's the friend of everyone in town except Mrs. Smathers. She says he's a pest."

Chester sighed. Mrs. Smathers tried to run the town, and she was against everything. Right now she was mostly against dinosaurs. One day Bronto had gone into her private driveway to avoid a fire truck, scaring her out of her wits. Mrs. Smathers had had a grudge against dinosaurs ever since.

"Mrs. Smathers is out to get Bronto," the mailman told Chester. "I heard her say that she was going to your house today to order him out of town."

Chester cried, "I'll have to hide Bronto!"

The mailman gazed up at the huge animal. "I can't imagine where!" he exclaimed.

"Oh, I have an idea where," said Chester, scrambling down to the ground.

"Well," said the mailman, "here's your package. And good luck!"

Chester hoped that Mr. Tubbs had sent something magic from a faraway place that would save Bronto from Mrs. Smathers. Quickly he tore open the package.

All that the package contained was a rug. It was a faded rug that looked like the old ones his mother used under porch furniture.

Chester had no time to wonder about the shabby rug. He sped to the porch and put it under his mother's red rocking chair. Then he mounted Bronto and rode rapidly away toward the pond outside of town.

At the pond Chester quickly dismounted.
Down from the dinosaur's back he slid.

Chester pointed to the water. "Get in there, Bronto, and hide," he ordered.

Obediently, Bronto waded into the pond and submerged until only his head and a bit of his long neck were sticking out.

"Don't let anyone see you," said Chester.

The dinosaur sank even lower in the water. Then Chester waved a reluctant good-by to Bronto and raced for home.

Mrs. Smathers was sitting on the porch in the red rocker when Chester got home. She was dressed all in black silk, and she was clutching a black silk umbrella.

Chester's mother was talking to her. "Now, Mrs. Smathers, Bronto never did any harm," said Mrs. Pokleberry. "He's a nice, clean animal. He obeys Chester."

Mrs. Smathers bent forward in her chair. "That doesn't concern me!" she snapped. "This petition does!"

She thrust a paper at Mrs. Pokleberry. Chester looked over his mother's shoulder to see what the paper said.

"BRONTO IS A PUBLIC NUISANCE. BRONTO MUST GO," it said. Beneath these words one hundred names were signed.

"B-b-but—" stammered Chester's mother, "these people don't even live in our town."

Grabbing the paper, Mrs. Smathers cried, "That's not the point. They might move here someday." And with that, she thumped her silken umbrella on the rug under the rocker.

Instantly the red rocker, with the rug
under it, skimmed over the porch rail and
went gliding into the air. Mrs. Smathers,
speechless with surprise, sat stiffly upright
in the chair.

Higher and higher soared the rocker.
Then it leveled off and sailed straight toward
the center of town.

Chester and his mother raced after it.

Soon the street was jammed with people
racing along, looking up at the strange sight.

"It's a dodo bird," cried one person.

"It's a flying saucer," said another.

"It's Mrs. Smathers!" yelled Chester.

The spectators gasped. Was this some new way that Mrs. Smathers had of running everyone's affairs?

When she sailed by the church, she reached out with her umbrella and hooked the handle around the church steeple. Then she started sailing around and around the steeple.

Some pigeons that had fluttered in panic from the belfry circled around the steeple, too. Mrs. Smathers, who was screaming for help, looked very much like a large black bird in distress.

Finally someone in the crowd of people on the ground said, "I do believe she can't get down!"

Someone else said, "When she gets tired of holding on to that umbrella, the wind will carry her to some other town."

"Splendid!" shouted almost everybody. "Then she can boss things somewhere else."

"Stop!" cried Chester's mother. "We must rescue her. Call the fire department. Tell the men to bring their ladders."

The firemen came and brought ladders. But they did not have a ladder that was long enough to reach Mrs. Smathers.

"Somebody might talk to her," suggested one of the firemen. "She probably has an idea how to get down. She has ideas about everything imaginable."

"I'll talk to her," volunteered Chester. Then he called very loudly, "Mrs. Smathers, can you hear me?"

Mrs. Smathers nodded.

"Do you have any idea how you can get down?" Chester shouted.

Mrs. Smathers shook her head violently.

"Well, I do!" Chester yelled. "But it requires Bronto's help. If we get you down, will you stop calling my dinosaur a public nuisance and hurting his feelings?"

Mrs. Smathers nodded again and dropped the paper with the names on it.

Someone in the crowd called, "Will you stop trying to boss everyone?"

"Yes! Yes!" shouted Mrs. Smathers.

Chester brought Bronto to the church.

Quickly he climbed up the dinosaur's neck, grabbed hold of the umbrella, and unhooked it from the church steeple.

Down Chester slid. Down he slid to the ground, towing Mrs. Smathers, the rocker, and the rug after him.

"Thank you for helping me," said Mrs. Smathers. "I know now that I have been the pest, not Bronto. From now on I'm going to try to be a pleasanter person and a nicer neighbor."

Then she added with a smile, "I'm going to be nicest of all to dinosaurs."

Questions

1. How did Chester get Bronto?

2. Do you think a dinosaur would make a good pet? Why, or why not?

3. Why did people dislike Mrs. Smathers? Do you think they will like her more or like her less after what happened in this story? Why?

4. On the second page of this book you can see things that happened in four of the stories in the book.

What story does each of the four pictures make you think of?

What You Know
about Words You Can Read

feel	solve	steeple	delight
sit	night	raisin	admit
corn	eat	eager	perform
those	day	weather	suppose
care	head	fountain	declare
kind	rain	royal	remind
shout	boy	poodle	revolve
boil	fault	autumn	avoid
now	boot	coward	reply
sky	learn	early	dismay

1. In which two lists are all the words one-syllable words? two-syllable words?

2. In which list of two-syllable words are all the words accented on the first syllable? the second syllable?

3. Look at the spelling of each one-syllable word and think about the vowel sound you hear. For each one-syllable word there is a two-syllable word that has the same vowel sound in the accented syllable and the same spelling for that vowel sound. Find each of these two-syllable words.

shatter	razor	planet
cinder	private	timid
public	pupil	study
passenger	stadium	lavender
principal	dinosaur	imitate

1. The first syllable is accented in all the words above. Which words in each list are two-syllable words? three-syllable words?

2. How many consonant letters follow the first vowel letter in each word in the first list? Do you hear long or short vowel sounds in the accented syllables of these words?

3. How many consonant letters follow the first vowel letter in each word in the second list? in the third list? In which list of words do you hear long vowel sounds in the accented syllables of all the words? short vowel sounds?

4. In which underlined word below do you hear a short vowel sound in the accented syllable? a long vowel sound?

My <u>family</u> likes to listen to the <u>radio.</u>

Alaska	kimono	examine
committee	potato	consider
tremendous	peculiar	delicious
reluctant	occasion	imagine
expression	commotion	petition

1. How many syllables do you hear in all the words above? Which syllable is accented in all the words?

2. How many consonant letters follow the second vowel letter in each word in the first list? Do you hear long or short vowel sounds in the accented syllables of these words?

3. How many consonant letters follow the second vowel letter in the words in the second list? in the third list? In which list of words do you hear long vowel sounds in the accented syllables? short vowel sounds?

4. In which underlined word below do you hear a short vowel sound in the accented syllable? a long vowel sound?

John is from North <u>Dakota</u>.

Bill is from <u>Kentucky</u>.

garden   carrot   errand

certain   parent   very

1. The two-syllable words above are accented on the first syllable. In which word do you hear the vowel of <u>car</u> in the accented syllable? the vowel of <u>her</u>? Why would you expect to hear these vowel sounds?

2. Do you hear the vowel of <u>car</u> in the accented syllable of the word <u>carrot</u> or <u>parent</u>? Do you hear the vowel of <u>her</u> in the accented syllable of the word <u>errand</u> or <u>very</u>? Why would you not expect to hear these vowel sounds?

3. The words below have more than two syllables. Which are accented on the first syllable? the second? In which word do you hear the vowel of <u>car</u> in the accented syllable? the vowel of <u>her</u>? Why would you not expect to hear these vowel sounds in the accented syllables of the other words?

carpenter   parachute   terrible

emergency   embarrass   experiment

problem	valley	giant
program	palace	lion
April	altitude	fuel
acrobat	Baltimore	violent

1. All the words above are accented on the first syllable. How many consonant letters follow the first vowel letter in all the words in the first list? What are these consonant letters? In which two words do you hear a short vowel sound in the accented syllable? a long vowel sound?

2. Say the second list of words and look at the spellings. In which words do you hear the vowel of <u>hat</u> in the accented syllable? In which word do you hear the vowel of <u>salt</u> in the accented syllable?

3. There are two vowel letters together in each word in the third list. Which three words are two-syllable words? Which word is a three-syllable word? Does the first vowel letter in each word stand for a long or a short vowel sound?

volunteer

conversation

anniversary

California

1. The words above have two accented syllables. The first syllable in each word has a secondary or lighter accent. The third syllable in each word has a primary or stronger accent. Say the words and listen to the two accented syllables.

2. Look at the spelling of each word. In which words do you hear the vowel of <u>hot</u> in the syllable with secondary accent? the vowel of <u>hat</u>?

3. In which word do you hear the vowel of <u>deer</u> in the syllable with primary accent? the vowel of <u>age</u>? the vowel of <u>her</u>? the vowel of <u>corn</u>?

4. In which underlined word below do you hear the vowel of <u>oil</u> in the syllable with primary accent? the vowel of <u>see</u>?

The <u>Halloween</u> party <u>disappointed</u> us.

a   dis   fore   im   re   un

Because of the underlined word, each sentence below does not make sense. Add one of the prefixes above to each underlined word to make the sentence sound right.

The artist painted trees in the background and a horse in the ground.

I bought a new baseball to place the one I lost.

It is possible to see across the ocean.

The horses had gone stray and could not be found.

Because the patient is now well, the doctor has continued his visits.

Most people dislike obedient children.

Ed wrapped the package to see what was inside of it.

We eat breakfast in the noon.

The man was aware that his boat was leaking, so he kept on fishing.

A dog's front legs may be called his legs.

able   er   ship   th   ty   ward   y

The underlined words below do not sound right in the sentences. To make each one of these words sound right, add one of the suffixes at the top of the page.

A thick grow of bushes hid the fence.

I was seven in line for the show.

The brothers formed a partner and went into business.

This wobble old chair is not comfort.

Tim broke the propel on his toy airplane.

Six is more than twenty.

Friend grew between the two boys.

Traffic laws are for our safe.

Mr. Hall pointed sea to show us the ship he would soon sail on.

My uncle is a radio announce.

We had an enjoy time at the party.

Abner Toggle wore out his flour sift.

The weather is rain and disagree.

William can do that dive back.

TO THE TEACHER

Purpose of the Book

The new *Tall Tales, Part Two*, is the fifth of the *Reading for Independence* books that accompany The New Basic Readers of the Curriculum Foundation Series. Children should use this book as soon as they have completed *More Roads to Follow*, Book Three, Part Two, of The New Basic Readers.[1]

The *Reading for Independence* books are designed specifically to provide an opportunity for each child to use interpretative and word-analysis skills simultaneously as he reads new material on his own.

Because the new *Tall Tales, Part Two*, is written largely in the familiar vocabulary of *More Roads to Follow*, children should be able to interpret the content fully. However, spaced judiciously among the familiar words are 412 new words—never more than nine to a page. These new words can be attacked independently by a child who has acquired the understandings and skills of word analysis taught in The New Basic Reading Program. If a child has acquired the abilities in interpretation and word analysis that are emphasized at Book Three, Part Two level, he grows significantly as he applies them while reading *Tall Tales, Part Two*.

Use of the Book

The stories in the new *Tall Tales, Part Two*, are designed to be read independently with little or no preliminary discussion or guidance. To encourage the child to think about what he has read, a few questions are placed after each story. Some of these questions check his interpretation of the story. Others focus attention on the word-analysis skills needed to identify the new words. In some instances, these questions may be used diagnostically. A pupil's response to these questions can reveal a great deal about his proficiency in interpretation and word analysis.

In the new *Tall Tales, Part Two*, the child uses structural analysis to attack new forms of words that he has met in The New Basic Readers and of words that he has already attacked in *Tall Tales, Part Two*. In this book the following words are counted as new forms and are printed in blue in the word list on pages 86-96:

words made by adding the prefix *fore* or *re* (*forehead, refold*)
words made by adding or dropping the suffix *able, ship, teen, th, ty,*
    or *ward*, with or without a spelling change (*imaginable, partnership, sixteen, fourth, specialty, skyward*)

To identify most of the new words in this book, the child must use phonetic analysis. In this book the child uses the following visual clues to vowel sounds in one-syllable words and in accented syllables of many words of more than one syllable:

[1]The New Basic Readers of the Curriculum Foundation Series, by Helen M. Robinson, Marion Monroe, A. Sterl Artley, and Charlotte S. Huck (Chicago: Scott, Foresman and Company).

a single vowel letter followed by one or more consonant letters other
than *r* (*snug, adjust*)

a single vowel letter followed by *r* (*fork, perform*)

a single vowel letter followed by one consonant letter and final *e* (*yoke,
amuse, introduce*)

a single vowel letter followed by *r* and final *e* (*blare, tore*)

a single vowel letter followed by two consonant letters and final *e*
(*grudge, solve*) or by *r*, another consonant letter, and final *e* (*swerve,
submerge*)

two vowel letters together (*rail, tray, beets, neat, coal, remain, dismay, steeple, repeat*)

two vowel letters together followed by *r* (*veer, soar, affair, volunteer*)

the letters *oi* or *oy* (*Roy, avoid, annoy*)

the letters *ou* (*grouch, fountain, announce*)

the letter *a* followed by *u* or *w* (*scrawl, autumn*)

spellings that represent
    the vowel of *boot* as in *nuisance*
    the vowel of *ice* as in *hind*
    the vowel of *go* as in *fold, jolt*

The child will need to use context clues to determine the vowel sound
that each of the following combinations of letters may represent:
oo as in *proof, poodle* and *hoof, crooked*
ow as in *bowl* and *vowel*
ea as in *dread*
ear as in *search*

To identify many of the new words of more than one syllable in this book,
the child uses the following spelling patterns as clues to vowel sound in
an accented first or second syllable:

A single vowel letter followed by more than one consonant letter usually
represents a short vowel sound (*package, milliner, reluctant*). If the first
of the consonant letters is *r*, the vowel sound is usually *r*-controlled
(*barber, carpenter, department*).

A single vowel letter followed by one consonant letter may be a clue to
a long vowel sound (*razor, dinosaur, commotion*) or to a short vowel
sound (*planet, lavender, imagine*).

In words ending in the letters *le* preceded by two consonant letters, a
single vowel letter usually represents a short vowel sound (*simple,
assemble*). If the first of the two consonant letters is *r*, the vowel sound
is usually *r*-controlled (*sparkle*).

In words ending in the letters *le* preceded by one consonant letter, a
single vowel letter usually represents a long vowel sound (*maple, noble*).

A single vowel letter followed by consonant letters that represent a
consonant blend may stand for a long vowel sound (*April, program*).

Two vowel letters together may represent two syllables, the first of the
two vowel letters usually representing a long vowel sound (*fuel, violent*).

The letter *a* or *e* followed by two *r*'s or one *r* and a vowel letter is a clue
to the vowel of *care* or *let* (*narrow, parachute, embarrass; errand, experiment*).

The letter *a* followed by *l* more often represents the vowel of *hat* than the vowel of *salt* (*gallon, altitude*).

In the new *Tall Tales, Part Two*, the child must also combine structural and phonetic analysis to attack inflected and derived forms of unknown words of one or more syllables, with or without spelling changes before the affix. For example, he attacks the new word *marvelous* by first using structural analysis to note that this is a root word plus the suffix *ous* and then by noting the spelling pattern that is a clue to an *r*-controlled vowel sound in the initial accented syllable of *marvel*. He also attacks compounds like *soapsuds* in which one root is an unknown printed word or like *spick-and-span* in which two roots are unknown printed words. He analyzes the unknown roots in these compounds (*suds, spick, span*) by noting the visual clue to short vowel sounds.

Since the child must use word analysis to identify the new words in this book, it is recommended that you stop to reteach a skill or understanding with which he shows any difficulty.

Perhaps all the reteaching that is required can be done by working with the child through specific pages in the section called "What You Know about Words You Can Read" (pages 75-83). Pages 76-81 provide a brief review of spelling patterns that function as clues to vowel sound in one-syllable words and in accented syllables of words of more than one syllable. Pages 82-83 review known prefixes and suffixes and understandings of structural analysis.

If you decide that a child needs further practice in the skills basic to word analysis, you will find many suggestions for help in specific exercises listed in the Index of Skills in the *Guidebooks* to accompany The New Basic Readers.

A few minutes spent in discussing with children the features of the new *Tall Tales, Part Two*, will encourage confidence in using the book independently. As pupils leaf through the pages of *Tall Tales*, call attention to the questions that appear after each story. Then ask pupils to turn to page 75. Explain briefly how the pages of this section, "What You Know about Words You Can Read," will help pupils in their reading.

LIST OF ATTACK WORDS

The 412 words in the following list can be attacked at this level by structural or phonetic analysis or by a combination of both skills. The 15 words printed in blue can be attacked through structural analysis.

After each attack word the method of analysis used to identify the word is indicated in parentheses.[1] A word that is used as a basis for structural analysis is printed in italics after the parentheses only if it is a word attacked previously in this book. The starred words in this list were used in the new *We Three*, in the new *What Next? Part One*, in the new *What Next? Part Two*, or in the new *Tall Tales, Part One*, the first four *Reading for Independence* books, but not in *More Roads to Follow*.

[1]The vowel sounds in words like *boss* and *solve* and in the accented syllables of words like *coffee, nuisance,* and *introduce* vary regionally. Your pupils will of course use the pronunciation to which they are accustomed.

1 tales* (visual clue to long vowel sound)

Flyaway at the Air Circus

4 circus* (visual clue to *r*-controlled vowel sound in accented syllable)
airport (compound; port—visual clue to *r*-controlled vowel sound)
skyward (known root +suffix)
passenger (visual clue to short vowel sound in accented syllable)
factory (visual clue to short vowel sound in accented syllable)
events (visual clue to short vowel sound in accented syllable)

5 sped* (visual clue to short vowel sound)
pump (visual clue to short vowel sound)
jet (visual clue to short vowel sound)
performing (root +ending; perform —visual clue to *r*-controlled vowel sound in accented syllable)
parachute (visual clue to vowel sound in accented syllable)
army (visual clue to *r*-controlled vowel sound in accented syllable)
stunts* (visual clue to short vowel sound)

6 bounced* (root with final *e* dropped +ending; bounce—visual clue to vowel sound)
rudder (visual clue to short vowel sound in accented syllable)
altitude (context to determine vowel sound in accented syllable)
marvelous (root +suffix; marvel— visual clue to *r*-controlled vowel sound in accented syllable)
propel (visual clue to short vowel sound in accented syllable)

7 gas (visual clue to short vowel sound)
tank (visual clue to short vowel sound)
throbbed (root with final consonant doubled +ending; throb—visual clue to short vowel sound)
lessons (visual clue to short vowel sound in accented syllable)

spiraling (root +ending; spiral— context to determine vowel sound in accented syllable)
diving (root with final *e* dropped + ending; dive—visual clue to long vowel sound)
dreadfully (root +suffixes; dread— context to determine vowel sound)

8 squiggles (visual clue to short vowel sound in accented syllable)
moaned (root +ending; moan— visual clue to long vowel sound)
horrible (visual clue to *r*-controlled vowel sound in accented syllable)
depressed (root +ending; depress— visual clue to short vowel sound in accented syllable)
tremendous (visual clue to short vowel sound in accented syllable)

9 streaked (root +ending; streak— visual clue to long vowel sound)
zoomed (root +ending; zoom—context to determine vowel sound)
poodle (context to determine vowel sound in accented syllable)

10 socks* (visual clue to short vowel sound)
pajamas (context to determine vowel sound in accented syllable)
pipe* (visual clue to long vowel sound)
wisp (visual clue to short vowel sound)
hangar (visual clue to short vowel sound in accented syllable)
forlorn (visual clue to *r*-controlled vowel sound in accented syllable)
hired* (root with final *e* dropped + ending; hire—visual clue to long vowel sound)

11 remained (root +ending; remain —visual clue to long vowel sound in accented syllable)
hurray (visual clue to long vowel sound in accented syllable)
wreath (visual clue to long vowel sound)
kissed* (root +ending; kiss—visual clue to short vowel sound)

12 drain (visual clue to long vowel sound)

accented (root +ending; accent—visual clue to short vowel sound in accented syllable)

vowel (context to determine vowel sound in accented syllable)

William

13 grouch (visual clue to vowel sound)

admired* (root with final e dropped +ending; admire—visual clue to long vowel sound in accented syllable)

14 stylish (root with final e dropped +suffix; style—visual clue to long vowel sound)

sir* (visual clue to r-controlled vowel sound)

squinted (root +ending; squint—visual clue to short vowel sound)

britches (visual clue to short vowel sound in accented syllable)

vest (visual clue to short vowel sound)

butt (visual clue to short vowel sound)

shallow (context to determine vowel sound in accented syllable)

ditch* (visual clue to short vowel sound)

15 tossing* (root +ending; toss—visual clue to short vowel sound)

milliner (visual clue to short vowel sound in accented syllable)

lavender (context to determine vowel sound in accented syllable)

weather-vane (compound; vane—visual clue to long vowel sound)

tapped* (root with final consonant doubled +ending; tap—visual clue to short vowel sound)

dimpled (root with final e dropped +ending; dimple—visual clue to short vowel sound in accented syllable)

satin* (context to determine vowel sound in accented syllable)

velvet (visual clue to short vowel sound in accented syllable)

dumped* (root +ending; dump—visual clue to short vowel sound)

16 carpenter (visual clue to r-controlled vowel sound in accented syllable)

demanded (root +ending; demand—visual clue to short vowel sound in accented syllable)

snorted* (root +ending; snort—visual clue to r-controlled vowel sound)

fourth (known root +suffix)

forehead (known root +prefix)

flour (visual clue to vowel sound)

raisin (visual clue to long vowel sound in accented syllable)

custard (visual clue to short vowel sound in accented syllable)

wedding* (root with final consonant doubled +ending; wed—visual clue to short vowel sound)

17 expression (visual clue to short vowel sound in accented syllable)

bellowed (root +ending; bellow—visual clue to short vowel sound in accented syllable)

amused (root with final e dropped +ending; amuse—visual clue to long vowel sound in accented syllable)

request (visual clue to short vowel sound in accented syllable)

odd* (visual clue to short vowel sound)

sturdy (visual clue to r-controlled vowel sound in accented syllable)

specialty (known root +suffix)

18 suffix* (visual clue to short vowel sound in accented syllable)

prefix* (context to determine vowel sound in accented syllable)

The Palace Mystery

19 mystery (visual clue to short vowel sound in accented syllable)

spectacles (visual clue to short vowel sound in accented syllable)

Sundays (visual clue to short vowel sound in accented syllable)

occasions (context to determine vowel sound in accented syllable)

scribbles (visual clue to short vowel sound in accented syllable)

scrawls (visual clue to vowel sound)

twisted (root +ending; twist—visual clue to short vowel sound)

20 servant (visual clue to *r*-controlled vowel sound in accented syllable)
law (visual clue to vowel sound)
commas (visual clue to short vowel sound in accented syllable)
remarked (root +ending of known form *remarkable*)
dots (visual clue to short vowel sound)
heaved (root with final *e* dropped + ending; heave—visual clue to long vowel sound)
noblemen (compound; noble—visual clue to long vowel sound in accented syllable)
assemble (visual clue to short vowel sound in accented syllable)
commanded (root +ending; command—visual clue to short vowel sound in accented syllable)

21 studied (root with final *y* changed to *i* +ending; study—context to determine vowel sound in accented syllable)
magnifying (root +ending; magnify—visual clue to short vowel sound in accented syllable)
ink (visual clue to short vowel sound)
scorched (root +ending; scorch—visual clue to *r*-controlled vowel sound)
brilliant (visual clue to short vowel sound in accented syllable)
unreadable (known root +prefix and suffix)
clerk* (visual clue to *r*-controlled vowel sound)
drugstore (compound; drug—visual clue to short vowel sound)
pills (visual clue to short vowel sound)

22 delay (visual clue to long vowel sound in accented syllable)
reappeared (known word +prefix)
cents* (visual clue to short vowel sound)
prescription (visual clue to short vowel sound in accented syllable)
dose (visual clue to long vowel sound)

blare (visual clue to *r*-controlled vowel sound)
trumpets (visual clue to short vowel sound in accented syllable)

23 mercy* (visual clue to *r*-controlled vowel sound in accented syllable)
solved (root with final *e* dropped + ending; solve—visual clue to short vowel sound)
mint (visual clue to short vowel sound)

24 dismay (visual clue to long vowel sound in accented syllable)
Tilly (visual clue to short vowel sound in accented syllable)
confessed (root +ending; confess—visual clue to short vowel sound in accented syllable)

25 confused (root with final *e* dropped +ending; confuse—visual clue to long vowel sound in accented syllable)
receive (visual clue to long vowel sound in accented syllable)
astounded (root +ending; astound—visual clue to vowel sound in accented syllable)

Cassy's Idea

26 Cassy's (visual clue to short vowel sound in accented syllable)
Tuttle (visual clue to short vowel sound in accented syllable)
Elmer (visual clue to short vowel sound in accented syllable)
errand (visual clue to vowel sound in accented syllable)
Felix (context to determine vowel sound in accented syllable)
Hugo (context to determine vowel sound in accented syllable)

27 yoke (visual clue to long vowel sound)
hitch* (visual clue to short vowel sound)
radishes (context to determine vowel sound in accented syllable)
tomatoes (context to determine vowel sound in accented syllable)
beets (visual clue to long vowel sound)

purse (visual clue to r-controlled vowel sound)

28 gorgeous (visual clue to r-controlled vowel sound in accented syllable)

knots (visual clue to short vowel sound)

rig (visual clue to short vowel sound)

blame (visual clue to long vowel sound)

tug* (visual clue to short vowel sound)

giddap (visual clue to short vowel sound in accented syllable)

29 ruts (visual clue to short vowel sound)

jolt (visual clue to vowel sound)

smacked* (root +ending; smack—visual clue to short vowel sound)

bony (root with final e dropped + suffix; bone*—visual clue to long vowel sound)

hind (visual clue to vowel sound)

whoa (visual clue to long vowel sound)

clung (visual clue to short vowel sound)

30 hoofs (context to determine vowel sound)

stirred* (root with final consonant doubled +ending; stir—visual clue to r-controlled vowel sound)

suffocated (root with final e dropped +ending; suffocate—visual clue to short vowel sound in accented syllable)

31 haw (visual clue to vowel sound)

ages (visual clue to long vowel sound)

swerved (root with final e dropped +ending; swerve—visual clue to r-controlled vowel sound)

narrowly (root +suffix; narrow—visual clue to vowel sound in accented syllable)

pleaded (root +ending; plead—visual clue to long vowel sound)

jouncing (root with final e dropped +ending; jounce—visual clue to vowel sound)

smashed* (root +ending; smash—visual clue to short vowel sound)

scooting* (root +ending; scoot—context to determine vowel sound)

32 curved (root with final e dropped +ending; curve—visual clue to r-controlled vowel sound)

veered (root +ending; veer—visual clue to r-controlled vowel sound)

gee (visual clue to long vowel sound)

main* (visual clue to long vowel sound)

barber* (visual clue to r-controlled vowel sound in accented syllable)

commotion (context to determine vowel sound in accented syllable)

razor (context to determine vowel sound in accented syllable)

coal* (visual clue to long vowel sound)

33 skidded (root with final consonant doubled +ending; skid—visual clue to short vowel sound)

spluttered (root +ending; splutter—visual clue to short vowel sound in accented syllable)

regained (root +prefix and ending; gain—visual clue to long vowel sound)

strength (visual clue to short vowel sound)

scales (visual clue to long vowel sound)

34 temper (visual clue to short vowel sound in accented syllable)

crazy (context to determine vowel sound in accented syllable)

thirty (visual clue to r-controlled vowel sound in accented syllable)

The Rocket That Ran Away

35 rocket* (visual clue to short vowel sound in accented syllable)

April (context to determine vowel sound in accented syllable)

deserted (root +ending; desert—visual clue to r-controlled vowel sound in accented syllable)

bench* (visual clue to short vowel sound)

unfolded (root +prefix and ending; fold*—visual clue to vowel sound)

Mars* (visual clue to *r*-controlled vowel sound)

planets (context to determine vowel sound in accented syllable)

horrified (root with final *y* changed to *i*+ending; horrify—visual clue to *r*-controlled vowel sound in accented syllable)

36 timid-looking (compound; timid —context to determine vowel sound in accented syllable)

stuttered (root+ending; stutter— visual clue to short vowel sound in accented syllable)

refolded (known root+prefix and ending) *fold*

objected (root+ending; object— visual clue to short vowel sound in accented syllable)

nervous (root with final *e* dropped +suffix; nerve—visual clue to *r*-controlled vowel sound)

snugly (root+suffix; snug—visual clue to short vowel sound)

37 coffee (visual clue to short vowel sound in accented syllable)

orange* (visual clue to *r*-controlled vowel sound in accented syllable)

lettuce (visual clue to short vowel sound in accented syllable)

sipping* (root with final consonant doubled+ending; sip—visual clue to short vowel sound)

relaxing (root+ending; relax—visual clue to short vowel sound in accented syllable)

38 blushed (root+ending; blush— visual clue to short vowel sound)

shame* (visual clue to long vowel sound)

crime (visual clue to long vowel sound)

thousands* (visual clue to vowel sound in accented syllable)

enjoyable (known word+suffix)

avoid (visual clue to vowel sound in accented syllable)

embarrasses (visual clue to vowel sound in accented syllable)

39 distinctly (root+suffix; distinct —visual clue to short vowel sound in accented syllable)

acrophobia (visual clue to short vowel sound in first accented syllable; context to determine vowel sound in second accented syllable)

suffer (visual clue to short vowel sound in accented syllable)

unbelievable (known root with final *e* dropped+prefix and suffix)

succeed (visual clue to long vowel sound in accented syllable)

page* (visual clue to long vowel sound)

More Is Better

40 Abner (visual clue to short vowel sound in accented syllable)

Toggle (visual clue to short vowel sound in accented syllable)

marmalade (visual clue to *r*-controlled vowel sound in accented syllable)

treat* (visual clue to long vowel sound)

sprang* (visual clue to short vowel sound)

shelf* (visual clue to short vowel sound)

simple* (visual clue to short vowel sound in accented syllable)

yeast* (visual clue to long vowel sound)

batch (visual clue to short vowel sound)

41 sift (visual clue to short vowel sound)

bowl* (context to determine vowel sound)

rise (visual clue to long vowel sound)

rose* (visual clue to long vowel sound)

plump* (visual clue to short vowel sound)

loaves (root with *f* changed to *v* before ending; loaf*—visual clue to long vowel sound)

greased (root with final *e* dropped +ending; grease—visual clue to long vowel sound)

42 rap (visual clue to short vowel sound)

sold* (visual clue to vowel sound)

neglected (root +ending; neglect—
visual clue to short vowel sound
in accented syllable)

disgusted (root +ending; disgust—
visual clue to short vowel sound
in accented syllable)

imagine (context to determine vowel sound in accented syllable)

annoyed (root +ending; annoy—
visual clue to vowel sound in
accented syllable)

retorted (root +ending; retort—visual clue to r-controlled vowel
sound in accented syllable)

slam* (visual clue to short vowel
sound)

fuel (visual clue to long vowel
sound in accented syllable)

43 screen (visual clue to long vowel sound)

tramp (visual clue to short vowel
sound)

starved* (root with final e dropped
+ending; starve—visual clue to
r-controlled vowel sound)

slice (visual clue to long vowel
sound)

generous (context to determine
vowel sound in accented syllable)

Frank (visual clue to short vowel
sound)

Twitter (visual clue to short vowel
sound in accented syllable)

lend* (visual clue to short vowel
sound)

44 sixteen (known root +suffix)

delicious (context to determine
vowel sound in accented syllable)

odor (context to determine vowel
sound in accented syllable)

braked* (root with final e dropped
+ending; brake—visual clue to
long vowel sound)

bicycles (context to determine vowel sound in accented syllable)

vans (visual clue to short vowel
sound)

45 scrap (visual clue to short vowel sound)

fountain (visual clue to vowel sound
in accented syllable)

flocking (root +ending; flock—visual clue to short vowel sound)

46 partners (visual clue to r-controlled vowel sound in accented
syllable)

success (visual clue to short vowel
sound in accented syllable)

partnership (known root +suffix)
partner

requires (visual clue to long vowel
sound in accented syllable)

cinders (visual clue to short vowel
sound in accented syllable)

47 admitted (root with final consonant doubled +ending; admit—
visual clue to short vowel sound
in accented syllable)

sentences* (visual clue to short
vowel sound in accented syllable)

Westley Riggs Thinks

48 Westley (visual clue to short
vowel sound in accented syllable)

Riggs (visual clue to short vowel
sound)

repeated (root +ending; repeat—
visual clue to long vowel sound
in accented syllable)

Marble* (visual clue to r-controlled
vowel sound in accented syllable)

grade (visual clue to long vowel
sound)

search* (context to determine vowel sound)

program (context to determine vowel sound in accented syllable)

gym (visual clue to short vowel
sound)

pupils (context to determine vowel
sound in accented syllable)

49 spick-and-span (compound;
spick, span—visual clue to short
vowel sound)

greet* (visual clue to long vowel
sound)

crooked (root +ending; crook—context to determine vowel sound)

zigzag (visual clue to short vowel
sound in accented syllables)

Roy (visual clue to vowel sound)

Burd (visual clue to r-controlled
vowel sound)

tumbled* (root with final *e* dropped +ending; tumble—visual clue to short vowel sound in accented syllable)

imitating (root with final *e* dropped +ending; imitate—context to determine vowel sound in accented syllable)

50 hissed* (root +ending; hiss—visual clue to short vowel sound)

Sarahlee (compound name; lee—visual clue to long vowel sound)

Martin (visual clue to *r*-controlled vowel sound in accented syllable)

entire (visual clue to long vowel sound in accented syllable)

51 ridiculous (context to determine vowel sound in accented syllable)

announced* (root with final *e* dropped +ending; announce—visual clue to vowel sound in accented syllable)

rumpled (root with final *e* dropped +ending; rumple—visual clue to short vowel sound in accented syllable)

behave (visual clue to long vowel sound in accented syllable)

platform (visual clue to short vowel sound in accented syllable)

baton (visual clue to short vowel sound in accented syllable)

dismissed (root +ending; dismiss—visual clue to short vowel sound in accented syllable)

52 stage (visual clue to long vowel sound)

whoops (context to determine vowel sound)

emergency (visual clue to *r*-controlled vowel sound in accented syllable)

principal (visual clue to short vowel sound in accented syllable)

definitely (root +suffix; definite—context to determine vowel sound in accented syllable)

acrobat (visual clue to short vowel sound in accented syllable)

mumbled (root with final *e* dropped +ending; mumble—visual clue to short vowel sound in accented syllable)

53 predicament (context to determine vowel sound in accented syllable)

54 conversation (visual clue to short vowel sound in first accented syllable; context to determine vowel sound in second accented syllable)

wobbled (root with final *e* dropped +ending; wobble—visual clue to short vowel sound in accented syllable)

thump* (visual clue to short vowel sound)

shadow (context to determine vowel sound in accented syllable)

bet* (visual clue to short vowel sound)

shrill (visual clue to short vowel sound)

55 flipped* (root with final consonant doubled +ending; flip—visual clue to short vowel sound)

character (visual clue to vowel sound in accented syllable)

The Machine

56 Fuddle (visual clue to short vowel sound in accented syllable)

press* (visual clue to short vowel sound)

brain (visual clue to long vowel sound)

bragged* (root with final consonant doubled +ending; brag—visual clue to short vowel sound)

57 anniversary (visual clue to short vowel sound in first accented syllable; visual clue to *r*-controlled vowel sound in second accented syllable)

experiment (visual clue to vowel sound in accented syllable)

brand-new (compound; brand—visual clue to short vowel sound)

purchase (visual clue to *r*-controlled vowel sound in accented syllable)

wrenches (visual clue to short vowel sound)

93

hammers (visual clue to short vowel sound in accented syllable)

files (visual clue to long vowel sound)

cogwheels (compound; cog—visual clue to short vowel sound)

sixty (known root +suffix)

58 introduce (visual clue to short vowel sound in first accented syllable; visual clue to long vowel sound in second accented syllable)

pride* (visual clue to long vowel sound)

59 proof (context to determine vowel sound)

skill (visual clue to short vowel sound)

mashed* (root +ending; mash—visual clue to short vowel sound)

gravy (context to determine vowel sound in accented syllable)

chocolate (context to determine vowel sound in accented syllable)

maple-nut (compound; maple—visual clue to long vowel sound in accented syllable)

cheese (visual clue to long vowel sound)

stack* (visual clue to short vowel sound)

garbage* (visual clue to r-controlled vowel sound in accented syllable)

60 groan* (visual clue to long vowel sound)

safety (known root +suffix)

fret* (visual clue to short vowel sound)

sparkling (root with final e dropped +ending; sparkle—visual clue to r-controlled vowel sound in accented syllable)

inquired* (root with final e dropped +ending; inquire—visual clue to long vowel sound in accented syllable)

sanitary (context to determine vowel sound in first accented syllable; visual clue to vowel sound in second accented syllable)

tray (visual clue to long vowel sound)

rattling* (root with final e dropped +ending; rattle—visual clue to short vowel sound in accented syllable)

clanking* (root +ending; clank—visual clue to short vowel sound)

61 shattered (root +ending: shatter—visual clue to short vowel sound in accented syllable)

opposite (visual clue to short vowel sound in accented syllable)

foaming (root +ending; foam—visual clue to long vowel sound)

soapsuds (compound; suds—visual clue to short vowel sound)

gallons (context to determine vowel sound in accented syllable)

62 adjusted (root +ending; adjust—visual clue to short vowel sound in accented syllable)

gleaming (root +ending; gleam—visual clue to long vowel sound)

neat* (visual clue to long vowel sound)

forks (visual clue to r-controlled vowel sound)

spoons (context to determine vowel sound)

clanging (root +ending; clang—visual clue to short vowel sound)

screeched* (root +ending; screech—visual clue to long vowel sound)

clog (visual clue to short vowel sound)

63 ruined (root +ending; ruin—visual clue to vowel sound in accented syllable)

heap* (visual clue to long vowel sound)

trash (visual clue to short vowel sound)

bin (visual clue to short vowel sound)

64 choose (context to determine vowel sound)

Chester's Pet

65 Chester's (visual clue to short vowel sound in accented syllable) glorious (root with final *y* changed to *i* +suffix; glory*—visual clue to *r*-controlled vowel sound in accented syllable)

autumn (visual clue to vowel sound in accented syllable)

Bronto (visual clue to short vowel sound in accented syllable)

dinosaur (context to determine vowel sound in accented syllable)

Pokleberry (compound name; Pokle —visual clue to long vowel sound in accented syllable)

Tubbs (visual clue to short vowel sound)

traveling (root +ending; travel— context to determine vowel sound in accented syllable)

66 rare (visual clue to *r*-controlled vowel sound)

exist (visual clue to short vowel sound in accented syllable)

package* (visual clue to short vowel sound in accented syllable)

Smathers (visual clue to short vowel sound in accented syllable)

pest* (visual clue to short vowel sound)

private (context to determine vowel sound in accented syllable)

grudge (visual clue to short vowel sound)

67 scrambling (root with final *e* dropped +ending; scramble—visual clue to short vowel sound in accented syllable)

tore* (visual clue to *r*-controlled vowel sound)

contained (root +ending; contain— visual clue to long vowel sound in accented syllable)

faded (root with final *e* dropped + ending; fade—visual clue to long vowel sound)

furniture (visual clue to *r*-controlled vowel sound in accented syllable)

shabby (visual clue to short vowel sound in accented syllable)

mounted (root +ending; mount— visual clue to vowel sound)

rapidly (root +suffix; rapid—context to determine vowel sound in accented syllable)

68 obediently (root +suffix; obedient—context to determine vowel sound in accented syllable)

waded* (root with final *e* dropped +ending; wade—visual clue to long vowel sound)

submerged (root with final *e* dropped +ending; submerge—visual clue to *r*-controlled vowel sound in accented syllable)

reluctant (visual clue to short vowel sound in accented syllable)

69 clutching (root +ending; clutch —visual clue to short vowel sound)

umbrella (visual clue to short vowel sound in accented syllable)

concern (visual clue to *r*-controlled vowel sound in accented syllable)

petition (context to determine vowel sound in accented syllable)

thrust (visual clue to short vowel sound)

public (visual clue to short vowel sound in accented syllable)

nuisance (visual clue to vowel sound in accented syllable)

stammered (root +ending; stammer —visual clue to short vowel sound in accented syllable)

70 skimmed (root with final consonant doubled +ending; skim— visual clue to short vowel sound)

rail (visual clue to long vowel sound)

gliding (root with final *e* dropped + ending; glide—visual clue to long vowel sound)

soared (root +ending; soar—visual clue to *r*-controlled vowel sound)

leveled (root +ending; level—context to determine vowel sound in accented syllable)

center* (visual clue to short vowel sound in accented syllable)

jammed* (root with final consonant doubled +ending; jam—visual clue to short vowel sound)

dodo (context to determine vowel sound in accented syllable)

saucer (visual clue to vowel sound in accented syllable)

71 spectators (visual clue to short vowel sound in accented syllable)

affairs (visual clue to *r*-controlled vowel sound in accented syllable)
steeple (visual clue to long vowel sound in accented syllable)

72 pigeons (context to determine vowel sound in accented syllable)
panic (context to determine vowel sound in accented syllable)
belfry (visual clue to short vowel sound in accented syllable)
distress (visual clue to short vowel sound in accented syllable)
splendid (visual clue to short vowel sound in accented syllable)
boss (visual clue to short vowel sound in accented syllable)

department (visual clue to *r*-controlled vowel sound in accented syllable)
imaginable (known root with final *e* dropped +suffix) *imagine*

73 volunteered (root +ending; volunteer—context to determine vowel sound in first accented syllable; visual clue to *r*-controlled vowel sound in second accented syllable)
violently (root +suffix; violent—visual clue to long vowel sound in accented syllable)
towing (root +ending; tow—context to determine vowel sound)

ACKNOWLEDGMENTS

For permission to adapt and use copyrighted material, grateful acknowledgment is made to the following:

To the author for "Flyaway at the Air Circus" by Leone Adelson from *Story Parade*, August 1948. To the publisher for "William" by Ernestine Cobern Beyer from *Humpty Dumpty's Magazine*, May 1957. To the publisher for "The Palace Mystery," adapted from "The Squiggly Writing" by Norman Hunter in *Child Life*, January 1939. To the author for "Cassy's Idea," adapted from "Elmer Tuttle's Wild Steer" by Kathryn Bilterman. To the author for "The Rocket That Ran Away" by Artie Jackson from *Young Elizabethan*, March 1958. To the author for "More Is Better," adapted from "Grandpa Toggle's Wonderful Bread" in *Grandpa Toggle's Wonderful Book* by Robert L. Grimes. To the author and publisher for "Westley Riggs Thinks" by Polly Curren from *Child Life*, August-September and October 1955. To the author for "The Machine" by Ruth Stempel. To the publisher for "Chester's Pet," adapted from "Chester and the Magic Rug" by Barbee Oliver Carleton in *Child Life*, August-September and October 1957.

Grateful acknowledgment is made to Lillian Gray for her contributions to earlier editions of the *Reading for Independence* books.